Dear Junior Gymnast:

My name is Dominique Dawes, and ever since I can remember I've loved to fly through the air. When I was really little, I used to do somersaults on the furniture in my house. My mom and dad signed me up for gymnastics because I had so much energy — and because they wanted to save their furniture!

I loved learning new tricks at the gym. But sometimes it was scary. When my coach, Kelli Hill, wanted me to do a back handspring on the high beam, I was afraid to even try it!

But I knew Kelli would never ask me to do something I wasn't ready to do. I thought about that great feeling in gymnastics of flying through the air and landing on two feet. I took a deep breath, set my mind to it, and tried the back handspring. And guess what? I didn't land on two feet the first time. Or the second time. But soon I did. And it felt great!

In this book, Katie Magee is afraid to go backward. Will she learn to get over being scared?

Enjoy the book!

Dominique Dawes

Read more books about the Junior Gymnasts!

Katie's Big Move

JUNIOR GYMNASTS

Katie's Big Move

BY TEDDY SLATER

illustrated by Wayne Alfano

A
LITTLE APPLE
PAPERBACK

SCHOLASTIC INC.
New York Toronto London Auckland Sydney

With special thanks to
Tom Manganiello of
57th Street Magic Gym.

A PARACHUTE PRESS BOOK

ISBN 0-590-85998-6

12 11 10 9 8 7 6 5 4 3 2 1   6 7 8 9/9 0 1/0

Printed in the U.S.A.   40

First Scholastic printing, June 1996

*For the real Lila — Lila Margulies
— with love.*

Contents

Katie's Big Move

★ 1
Backing Off

"Today we're going to learn a back walkover on the beam," Coach Jody announced on Monday afternoon.

"Yippee!" Dana Lewis yelled.

"All *riiight!*" Amanda Calloway cheered.

"Oh, no!" I said.

I hate going backward. Especially on the balance beam. It is *so* scary. You can't see where you're going. Just thinking about it makes me want to throw up!

"Don't worry, Katie," Dana whispered. "You can do it."

Katie — that's me. My whole name is Kathryn Mary Margaret Magee, but nobody ever calls me that. My mom says I'll grow into my name eventually. But sometimes I wonder. Right now, I'm the smallest girl on my gymnastics team. I'm also the youngest.

"I hope so," I whispered back. Dana knows how scared I am of backward moves. Every time we have to learn a new one, I'm always the last girl on the team to get it right.

Dana is the best gymnast on our team. At least she was until Amanda came along. Now I'm not sure *who* is best.

Dana is nine, one year older than me. She's in fourth grade at Lincoln Elementary School. I'm in third grade at George Washington. Dana and I have been in the same class at Jody's Gym ever since I was four. That's when I started gymnastics. We became friends at my first class, as soon as I saw Dana's hair. I asked her if we could trade, because I wanted red hair just like hers. Dana said no, but we've been friends ever since!

I looked from Dana to Amanda. Amanda was staring at the beam with a smile on her face. I could tell she couldn't wait to try a back walkover.

Amanda joined our team about a month ago when her family moved here to Springfield. She's a great gymnast! So far, she's won five medals in competitions.

Amanda is nine, just like Dana. She has perfect posture and perfect manners. Amanda is African-American. She has big brown eyes and long curly hair. Amanda is very polite. She actually says "please" and "thank you" to her friends.

But Amanda's not polite when it comes to gymnastics. She *really* wants to win! So does Dana. Amanda and Dana argue a lot about which one is the best. I think they're both great!

The other girls in my class are Liz Halsey, Emily Stone, and Hannah Rose Crenshaw. They are all fourth graders, and they all go to Dana's school.

Amanda and I are the only ones from George Washington Elementary. I'm glad Amanda moved to Springfield, because now I don't have to ride my bike to the gym alone! Amanda and I ride home from school together every day. And on Mondays, Wednesdays, and Thursdays, we ride to the gym.

Everyone on my team is a Level 5 gymnast. Gymnasts first start to compete when they reach Level 5. We don't just compete, though. We also learn moves the Level 6 gymnasts do — like the back walkover on the beam.

I was still worried about the new move

when Coach Jody said, "Before we begin, I have a special announcement."

Good! I thought. Anything to keep from going backward!

"I'm starting a program called Tumbling Buddies," Coach Jody explained. "Each girl in Level 5 will be paired with a girl from the Elite team. Once a week the older girl will help you work."

Wow! The Elite girls are super-fantastic gymnasts, and they go to all the big competitions. To become an Elite gymnast, you have to go through all the levels — up to Level 10! Most of the Elite girls in Jody's Gym are teenagers.

"Do you think Lila Hanks will be a Tumbling Buddy?" Dana asked me.

"I hope so!" I said.

Lila Hanks is the very best gymnast at Jody's Gym. She's always winning medals. Dana and I even saw her on TV once. She looked beautiful! Just like a movie star.

"I want Lila to be my Tumbling Buddy!" Dana called out.

"No fair," Amanda said. "*I* want Lila!"

Hannah Rose frowned at Amanda. "Well, you can't have her!" she said in her usual bossy way. "You just moved here."

I wanted Lila for my Tumbling Buddy, too. But Dana almost always gets what she wants. So does Amanda. And so does Hannah Rose! I was pretty sure one of them would get Lila.

Coach Jody held up a hand. "Calm down," she laughed. "*I'll* decide who the Tumbling Buddies are."

"When?" Dana asked.

"I'll let you know on Thursday," Coach Jody said. "The Elite girls will be here then. In the meantime, let's get to work!"

Oh, no! I didn't want class to start. We always begin with a twenty-minute warm-up. That usually seems like a long time. But today it was way too short. All I could think about was the new move on the beam. The backward move.

After warm-up we spent fifteen minutes working on the uneven parallel bars, half an hour on floor exercises, and another fifteen minutes on the vault. And then it was time for the beam.

"Okay!" Coach Jody said. "Are you all ready for those back walkovers on the beam?"

Everyone yelled "Yes!" Everyone but me.

"Let's see them on the floor first!" Coach Jody said.

Dana groaned. "We can all do back walkovers. Why do we have to show you again?"

"Because you can't run — " Coach Jody started to say.

"Before you can walk," we finished. Then we all giggled. "You can't run before you can walk" is one of Coach Jody's favorite sayings. It means our moves have to be perfect on the floor — where it's safer — before we can try them on the equipment.

One by one, we each did a back walkover. Everyone could do it. Even me! I'm very proud of my back walkover. It took me a long time to learn.

"Good going," Coach Jody said when everyone finished. "Now I'll demonstrate the walkover on the practice beam." My heart began to pound. I don't even like to *watch* people go backward!

A real balance beam is four feet high. The practice beam comes up only to my knees. The practice beam is less dangerous. But both kinds of beams are only four inches wide. It's easy to fall off them.

Coach Jody stepped up onto the practice beam. She held her arms out and got her balance. Then Coach Jody leaned back. She put her hands down on the beam about twelve inches behind her feet. Slowly she pulled her right leg up and over her head. Then her left leg. When both feet were back down on the beam, she stood up, threw out her arms, and smiled. "Ta-da!" she said.

"That looks like fun," Dana said. "Can I go first?"

Coach Jody stepped off the beam. "Okay, Dana," she said. "Everyone else line up."

Amanda jumped into line right behind Dana and Liz. Then she took a giant step back. "Come on, Katie," she called. "I saved you a place."

I shook my head quickly. Amanda looked disappointed. But I wasn't ready to try the back walkover. I moved to the end of the line.

Hannah Rose was the last person on line. She rolled her eyes when she saw me. "Scared?" she asked. As if she didn't know. Everyone on our team — except Amanda

— knows I'm afraid to go backward. It's embarrassing.

Dana climbed up onto the practice beam. I held my breath.

Coach Jody knelt on the mat next to the beam to make sure Dana didn't fall. That's called spotting.

Dana leaned back. I couldn't believe how calm she looked. I was worried that Dana would miss the beam. What if she fell? But she grabbed the beam firmly and pulled her legs over. Her walkover was a little wobbly, but she didn't fall.

Liz was next. She froze in the middle of the move and couldn't kick her legs over. That made me even *more* nervous. But after a few tries, Liz did it.

Amanda's back walkover was the best. She didn't wobble at all. I bet Amanda's not afraid of anything.

Emily went next. Coach Jody had to help her. But Emily didn't look scared.

When Hannah Rose's turn came, she hopped onto the beam and flipped right over. She wasn't as graceful as Amanda. But she was just as steady.

Now my heart was really pounding. I could hardly catch my breath!

I was next!

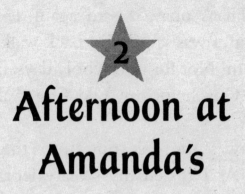

Afternoon at Amanda's

I took one slow step toward the beam. My legs felt shaky. My face felt hot. I knew it was bright red. I took another step.

Coach Jody suddenly jumped to her feet. "Oops!" she said. "We're late. I think we'd better start our cool-down now."

"But Katie didn't get her turn," Amanda called out.

"That's okay!" I said quickly.

Coach Jody smiled at me. "Sorry,

Katie," she said. "I promise you'll be first on Wednesday."

"That's okay," I said again. I couldn't believe it. I was saved! No back walkover on the beam! Not for two whole days. By then, maybe Coach Jody would forget all about me!

I was the last one into the locker room. As I tossed my sweaty leotard into my gym bag, I saw Amanda staring at me.

"What's the matter?" I asked. "You look funny." And she did. Her big brown eyes looked bigger than ever.

"Katie, are you mad at me?" Amanda whispered.

"Of course not!" I cried.

"Why wouldn't you stand next to me in line?" Amanda asked.

"Katie is scared to go backward," Dana blurted out before I could answer. "She didn't want to be at the front of the line."

"Dana!" I said. I couldn't believe she

said that. Everyone knows good gymnasts aren't afraid of anything. I felt my face get hot again.

Amanda stared at me. "Are you really scared?" she asked.

I nodded. "It took me three whole weeks to learn a backward roll. And I especially hate going backward on the beam!"

"But it's so easy," Amanda said.

"Not for me," I told her.

Amanda and Dana didn't say anything else for a while. Neither did I. But I wasn't feeling so happy anymore. Wednesday wasn't that far away.

After everyone changed, we went outside to the bike rack.

"You know what the Elite girls call a back walkover?" Dana asked as we pedaled slowly down Sixth Street.

"What?" Amanda asked.

"A flip-flop!" Dana said. Amanda giggled. I tried to smile, but I couldn't. I was afraid of the move no matter what they called it!

"Do you want me to help you?" Amanda asked.

"Really?" I said. "That would be great!" Maybe it wasn't so bad that Dana had told Amanda about my problem. Maybe Amanda could help me.

"Come over to my house right now," Amanda said. "We can practice on my beam."

Dana's mouth dropped open. "You have your own beam?" she cried. "Cool!"

Amanda shrugged. "It's not a *real* beam. My brother Peter made it for me. It's only a few inches off the ground."

"Good!" I said.

But Dana was frowning. "What if Katie falls off?" she said.

"She won't," Amanda answered. "Peter made the beam really wide. Mom thought it would be safer that way."

Dana moved her bicycle closer to mine. "I think you should let *me* help you," she said. "My plan is better than Amanda's."

"You have a plan?" I asked. "What is it?"

"Well . . ." Dana bit her lip. "I don't exactly have a plan yet. But I'll think of one."

We all stopped our bikes at the corner of Cranberry and Sixth. There's a big oak tree on that corner. We call it the Good-bye Tree. That's where Dana goes one way toward home. Amanda and I go another.

"Do you want to come over, too?" Amanda asked Dana.

"I can't," Dana said. "I have to watch Freddy."

Freddy is Dana's little brother. He's four. Dana watches him on the afternoons when her mother has to work. Mrs. Lewis writes sewing articles for *Pins and Needles* magazine.

"That's too bad," Amanda said. "You'll miss seeing how *my* plan works."

Dana frowned at Amanda. "I don't have to be there to know it's not going to work," she said.

Uh-oh, I thought. Dana and Amanda try to be good friends. But they like to compete with each other. Now they each wanted to come up with the best plan to help me.

"You can both help," I said quickly.

"Once I figure out *my* plan, you won't need Amanda's," Dana told me. Then she rode off down the street toward her house.

"We'll see!" Amanda called after her.

" 'Bye, Dana!" I yelled.

Dana waved, but she didn't say anything. I hoped she wasn't mad.

Amanda smiled at me. "Let's go!" she said. "We still have an hour before it gets dark."

"Okay," I said. A few minutes later we

turned into Amanda's driveway. I love going to her house!

Amanda's house is huge — just like her family. My parents are divorced and I don't have any brothers or sisters. So at my house, it's just me and Mom. Amanda likes *my* house because it's quiet. But I'd rather live in a noisy house like hers. Amanda has a great family — four kids, a mom and dad, one grandmother, and *seven* animals!

Amanda has a big sister, Gretchen, and a little sister, Gabriella. Then she has a big brother, Peter. Together, the Calloway kids have Tuna the cat, Polly and Golly the parrots, Hoppy and Happy the rabbits, Farfel the ferret, and a Great Dane puppy named Zelda.

I love animals. All kinds. When I grow up, I'm going to be a veterinarian. Or maybe a zookeeper. I'll have a million pets. Right now I just have a turtle named

Speedy. Speedy is great, but I wish he were a dog or a cat. I can't have either one, though, because they make my mom sneeze.

"Are you sure we're in the right place?" I asked as Amanda opened her front door. It seemed awfully quiet.

Just then, a giant ball of fur came galloping down the stairs. Zelda! She was wagging her tail so hard her whole backside moved.

"Hiya, girl!" I said. Zelda is so big she can lick my face without even jumping up.

"Yuck!" Amanda said, giggling. "Don't you hate it when she does that?"

I giggled, too. "Nope!" I said. "I love it!"

Amanda went over to the hall table and picked up a big pad of yellow paper.

"It's a note from my mom," Amanda said.

" 'Dear Mandy,' " she read out loud.
" 'Gone shopping. Gab's with me, Gretch is
at library, Pete at basketball, Gram upstairs
napping. Back soon. Love ya! Hugs. Mom.
P.S. More hugs!' "

I giggled. The note sounded just like
Amanda's mother. Mrs. Calloway always
talks very fast, and she never says anybody's
whole name. I guess when you have that
many kids, it saves time.

Amanda led me through the kitchen
and out the back door. "Hel-lo!" a screechy
voice called from the screened porch.

"Good-bye!" called an even screechier
one. It was only Polly and Golly. Or was it
Golly and Polly?

"Hel-lo!" Amanda yelled back.

"Good-bye!" I added.

I followed Amanda outside, down the
stone steps, and into the backyard. Zelda
stayed right at my heels.

The balance beam was in the middle of the yard. It was much lower and wider than a real beam — just like Amanda said.

"What if I fall?" I asked nervously.

"Don't worry. The grass is soft," Amanda said. "But you won't fall. I'll be spotting you."

"Well, okay," I said. "If you're sure." I stared at the beam and thought about doing a flip-flop. My stomach was doing flip-flops already! Slowly, I stepped up onto the beam.

"Ready?" Amanda asked.

"I guess so," I said. I made myself look at Amanda. I didn't want to think about the move. If I did, I would get even more scared.

"Well?" Amanda said. "What are you waiting for?"

I leaned back quickly before I could lose my nerve. The sky swirled above me. The clouds were upside down! I looked for the beam, but I couldn't see it. I couldn't see anything but sky. I was scared to lean back farther. I was scared to put my hands down. What if I missed the beam?

There was only one thing to do.

"Help!" I yelled.

3
Two Plans Too Many

"Katie!" Amanda said. "Take it easy!" She grabbed my right hand and guided it to the beam. I put my left hand down too.

"Are you okay?" Amanda asked.

"Uh-huh," I grunted. It was hard to talk in that position.

But I wasn't really okay. I felt dizzy. Everything was upside down. Amanda. The house. Even Zelda! I knew I was supposed to flip my legs up over my head. But I was too scared to move. I was stuck in a back bend on the beam!

"You're halfway there," Amanda said.

"All you have to do is kick up with your legs."

I tried. But nothing happened. It was as if someone had sneaked up and glued my feet to the beam. My legs weren't going anywhere.

My arms were getting tired. And my shoulders were starting to hurt. My back bend sank a little. I tried to push myself up into a nice curve. But I couldn't. I was too pooped. I sat down on the beam.

"What happened?" Amanda asked.

"I got scared," I said.

"Try again," Amanda ordered.

"No!" I climbed off the beam and sat in the grass. Zelda flopped down next to me. She put her head in my lap.

"That was horrible," I moaned.

Amanda sat on the beam. "It was a great back bend!"

"Yeah, well, I already know how to do those," I told her.

27

"Of course you do," Amanda said. "You can do lots of backward moves. I've seen you."

"I can *now*," I said. "But you weren't there when I was learning them. I got scared every time."

"I have a perfect idea," Amanda announced.

"What?" I asked.

"I'm going to make you relax about going backward!" Amanda said. Then she jumped up and ran toward the house.

"Where are you going?" I yelled after her.

"To get a piece of paper!" Amanda yelled back. "Come on!"

I followed Amanda up the stairs to her room. She sat down in her desk chair. I sat on her bed.

Amanda pulled a piece of pink paper out of her desk drawer. It was Monday — Amanda's pink day. She wears only one color at a time. And she has a color for every day of the week. But pink paper? I wondered if Amanda brought different-colored pens and notebooks to school every day. But I didn't ask.

"What are you doing?" I said instead.

"Making a list," Amanda replied. "Name all the backward moves you can do on the floor." She sounded excited.

I thought for a minute. "Um . . . back rolls, back bends, back walkovers," I finally said.

Amanda wrote everything down — with a pink pen! "I'm adding a backward roll-to-handstand and a back flip," she said.

"Actually, I'm not good at those yet," I said.

Amanda waved her hand as if that wasn't important. "Which moves do you like best?" she asked.

"None of them!" I said. "If they're backward, I hate them."

"Well, you have to learn to love them," Amanda insisted. "All of them. Then they won't be scary."

"How am I going to do that?" I asked.

"Do a hundred of each move every day," she said. "After a while the back walk-over on the beam will be easy!"

Amanda held out the list.

I just stared at her. I was glad she wanted to help me. But hundreds of backward moves a day? Yuck! Still, if Amanda thought it was a good idea, it probably was.

I took the list from her. "Okay," I said. "I'll try it."

"Dinner will be ready in five minutes," Mom said later that night. She closed the microwave door and pressed the Reheat button. "Why don't you put the tape in the VCR?" she suggested.

"Okay!" I agreed.

Mom and I usually eat a normal din-

30

ner at the kitchen table. But tonight we were having a party because Mom had won a big case. She's a lawyer. To celebrate, she brought home my favorite Chinese dinner — moo goo gai pan — my favorite dessert — marshmallow-brownie ice cream — and a new movie about a dog who saves lives.

I was just taking the video out of its box when the phone rang. I ran to get it. "Hello?"

"So how did it go at Amanda's?" It was Dana. She never says "Hello" on the phone.

"Not too good," I told her. "I got stuck in a back bend."

Dana giggled. "I guess Amanda's plan wasn't that great."

"It wasn't her fault," I said. "I was just too scared. Now she wants me to practice all the backward moves I know. She made me a list. I'm going to do each one a hundred times a day."

"A hundred times?" Dana repeated.

"That's crazy! You'd be going backward all day long. Know what you really should do?"

"What?"

"Work on your balance," she said.

"My balance?" I asked.

"Sure," Dana said. "That's what makes you afraid on the beam. You think you might fall off."

"I guess so," I said. "Maybe."

"Forget Amanda's plan," Dana told me. "Work on your balance instead."

"Katie! Dinner is ready!" Mom called out.

"I have to go eat," I told Dana.

"Okay," Dana said. "I'll see you on Wednesday."

I always like talking on the phone with Dana. But this time I wasn't sorry to hang up. I knew she wanted to help me. So did Amanda. But I was trying to forget about the backward move. And it was all they could talk about! I felt so nervous my stomach ached. Suddenly, that marshmallow-brownie ice cream didn't sound so good anymore.

★ 4

Disaster Number One

I planned to do each backward move on Amanda's list on Tuesday afternoon. But when I got home from school, there was a letter from my pen pal Amy Donahue. I have fourteen pen pals in eleven different countries. Amy lives in Sydney, Australia. She says Sydney is a gigantic city.

Amy was writing to tell me that her guinea pig had just had babies. Six of them! So of course I wrote back right away. I wanted to know what she named them all. The only trouble was, I couldn't find my pencil case. It's always disappearing.

Anyway, by the time I found my pencil case and finished the letter, dinner was ready. Then I did my math homework. Mom helped, so it took an extra long time. I had to explain a lot of stuff to her. Before I knew it, it was time for bed. And I hadn't done a single backward move.

The first thing I thought about when I woke up Wednesday morning was the back walkover. Right away, my toes began to tingle. That only happens when I'm worried about something big. I wasn't surprised. Doing a flip-flop on the beam is *gigantic*.

I went straight to the gym after school. Amanda and I usually go together. But I wanted to be super-early this time so I could practice the new move before class.

When I walked in, Coach Jody was in the gym with the Teeter Tots. That's her youngest class. The kids were rolling around on the floor and making lots of noise. I headed straight for the little gym.

The little gym is a room with a bunch of mats and a practice beam. I planned to try my back walkover in there — where nobody could see me. But when I pushed open the door, someone else was already inside.

It was Lila Hanks! She was working on her floor exercise. Lila almost never comes to the gym without the other Elite girls. They all practice at night. Coach Jody says it's because they need a peaceful atmosphere to work in. I didn't want to interrupt Lila, so I stood quietly in the doorway and watched her tumble.

Lila is amazing! She did a whole bunch of back flips and round-offs without stopping for a second. Her dark hair was pulled up, and her shiny blue leotard was beautiful. She looked just like an Olympic champion!

I sighed. Lila is so great. I bet *she* never had problems with something as easy as a back walkover on the beam.

The door opened behind me, and Hannah Rose came up next to me. She poked me in the ribs. "What are you doing here so early?" she asked.

"I wanted to practice," I said very, very quietly. I was afraid to bother Lila.

"Practice the new move on the beam?" Hannah Rose asked.

I nodded. "Shh!"

But there was no reason to whisper anymore. Lila had already finished her routine. Now she was stretching out.

"Watch this!" Hannah Rose told me. She marched right into the little gym and climbed onto the practice beam. Lila glanced up just as Hannah Rose did a back walkover.

My heart sank. Hannah Rose's walkover wasn't perfect. But it was *good* — much better than anything I could do.

Hannah Rose grinned as she climbed

off the beam. "Did you see my back walkover?" she asked Lila.

Lila smiled back. "I sure did," she said. "Looking good!"

"Thanks," Hannah Rose said sweetly. Then she turned to me. "Come on, Katie," she said in her bossiest voice, "Can't you see Lila is trying to practice?"

As if *I* were the one who was bothering her!

Hannah Rose can be such a pain!

I hurried into the locker room. Amanda was there, changing into her navy leotard. Wednesday is Amanda's blue day. Dana was getting dressed right next to her. Liz and Emily stood across the aisle.

Hannah Rose flopped down on the bench in front of Dana. "You can forget about Lila being your Tumbling Buddy," she said. "Coach Jody is going to give her to me."

"Why?" Dana demanded.

"Because Lila is the best gymnast in the Elite group," Hannah Rose said. "So Coach Jody will match her with the best gymnast on our team."

"That's right!" Dana said. "Me!"

"No — me!" Amanda cried.

Liz and Emily both laughed.

I didn't care who got Lila. The Teeter Tots were already walking into the locker room. That meant our class was about to start — and I would have to do the back walkover on the beam.

I got more and more nervous as we warmed up. My hands were shaking.

"We're going to begin with the beam today!" Coach Jody called. "Come on, Katie. You're up first!"

Why did she have to have such a good memory?

I walked slowly toward the beam. Suddenly the locker-room door opened.

40

Lila Hanks walked in. She began talking to Coach Jody. Great! I thought. I won't have to do the move until Lila leaves.

But Coach Jody waved me to the beam. "Come on, Katie!" she said. Lila smiled at me.

I couldn't believe it! I had to climb on the beam with Lila Hanks watching? Now I felt even more terrified! I glanced over at Amanda.

"Don't worry," she whispered. "Just think how much backward practicing you've done!"

I hadn't practiced at all. But I couldn't tell Amanda that. She would feel badly that I hadn't followed her plan.

"Don't think about going backward," Dana said. "Just think about your balance."

"Okay," I said. I thought about my balance. I thought, *What if I can't keep my balance?* This wasn't helping at all!

My throat felt dry as I mounted the

practice beam. I held my arms out for balance. The beam felt slippery under my feet.

Coach Jody moved over to spot me. She smiled. But I was too nervous to smile back.

"Can I do a front walkover first?" I asked.

"Sure," Coach Jody said. "Whatever makes you feel comfortable."

I did the front walkover.

"Good job!" Lila called. She was watching from behind Coach Jody. That made me feel better. Lila Hanks liked my walkover! Maybe I *could* do it backward!

I walked carefully to the end of the beam and pointed my right toe. With my arms over my head, I leaned back. I could see the walls of the gym. I could see Lila Hanks from the corner of my eye. But I couldn't see the beam. My feet were on it, but I didn't know where to put my hands. I knew I had to lean back farther. But I couldn't.

"Go for it!" Dana called out.

"Keep your toes pointed!" Amanda added.

I couldn't make myself go back any farther. I felt frozen in place. After a few seconds, I straightened up again.

"That's okay, Katie," Coach Jody said. "Just take a deep breath and try again."

I shook my head. "I can't," I whispered. "I'm too scared."

Lila Hanks frowned.

Dana and Amanda both looked surprised. But Hannah Rose didn't.

"Oh, Katie," Hannah Rose said. "Don't be such a scaredy-cat. I mean scaredy-*Kate*!" Then she giggled at her own joke.

I glanced down at Lila Hanks. She was smiling at me. Or maybe she was smiling at

Hannah Rose! Maybe Lila thought Hannah Rose was right. She thought I was a scaredy-cat!

I couldn't believe it. I had totally embarrassed myself in front of the best gymnast I knew! My face got hot. I couldn't stay on the beam for one more second.

"I'm too scared," I said again.

Then I jumped off the beam. And I ran for the locker room.

⭐ 5
Disaster Number Two

I raced down the steps in front of the gym. Amanda was right behind me. "You guys, wait up!" Dana called. She walked slowly, dragging her gym bag on the ground. It looked really heavy.

"Hurry," I called to her. I couldn't wait to get away from the gym — far away. And right away!

I unlocked my bike from the bike rack and waited for Dana.

"Want to come over to my house?" she asked. "We can work on your balance."

"No, come home with me," Amanda

said. "You can practice some more on my beam."

I shook my head. "I want to go home," I said. "I looked so wimpy! Lila Hanks thinks I'm a scaredy-cat!"

"No, she doesn't!" cried Amanda. "She probably just thinks you got nervous."

"Everybody gets nervous," Dana agreed. "Come on, let's go to my house. Once you practice your balance, you won't be scared anymore."

"She needs to practice going backward on my beam," Amanda argued. "That's what she's afraid of!"

I don't like it when my friends argue. "Let's all go someplace *together*," I told them.

"Okay," Amanda said. "Where?"

I thought quickly. "How about the park?" I suggested. It was halfway between Dana's and Amanda's houses.

"Sure," Dana said.

"Then let's go," I said. "I don't want Lila Hanks to see me again."

When we reached the park, I slumped down on the first bench I saw. Some little kids were playing in the sandbox. They looked like they were having fun.

"Little kids are so lucky," I said. "They're never afraid of falling."

"That's because they're so close to the ground!" Dana said.

"Yeah," Amanda agreed. "They don't have far to fall!"

They both looked at the little kids and laughed. Even I couldn't help smiling.

Amanda sat down next to me. "Do you want to practice your backward moves?" she asked.

"No," I said. "I'm still too scared from the gym."

"That's okay," Dana said. "*I* thought of a great plan to improve your balance." She sat on my other side and began digging through her gym bag.

Dana pulled an enormous book out of the bag. "Here," she said, handing it to me. "You just have to put this on your head. Then you balance it there while you walk. It's what models do."

"That won't work!" Amanda said.

"Yes it will!" Dana insisted.

Before Amanda could argue, I jumped up and put the book on my head. It fell off. I put it back on — and this time it stayed.

"Now walk," Dana said. I tried. But it wasn't easy. The book kept slipping to the side.

Dana and Amanda giggled.

So did I. Laughing made balancing even harder. I finally managed it, though. I walked slowly and carefully toward the sandbox. The little kids watched me with big eyes.

Suddenly, Amanda jumped up off the bench. "Hey, that's not a bad idea," she said. "But you should be doing it backward!"

I know I said I hate to do *anything* backward. But even I'm not afraid of just walking that way. I didn't really see how it would help. But I was glad Amanda and Dana were finally getting along.

Keeping my head straight, I took one step backward. And another. I was doing okay. I began to feel a little less awful.

Dana waved at me to stop. "I have an even better idea," she announced. "Just walking backward won't do anything. You should try walking on the side of the sand-box. It's skinny — just like a balance beam. But it's practically on the ground.

"That *is* a good idea," Amanda cried. "But do it backward!"

"I don't know," I said doubtfully. I was beginning to feel a little silly.

"Come on, Katie," Dana urged. "I know this will work."

As I climbed onto the side of the sandbox, the little kids scooted over to watch. "What are you going to do now?" a girl in red overalls wanted to know.

"A terrific trick," Dana told her. She held the book out to me. I took the book and balanced it on my head. I was getting good at that part! Then I started walking along the side of the sandbox. Backward!

"It's falling! It's falling!" the girl in red squealed. She sounded thrilled.

I held my head sideways to keep the book balanced. The more it slid, the more I tilted my head. I was so busy thinking about the book that I forgot about going backward. I just did it.

"Hey, Katie!" Dana sounded excited. "You're doing great! You're walking so fast!"

"And so *backward*!" Amanda added.

They were right! I raised both my fists in the air. "Hurray!" I hollered.

That's when I saw Lila Hanks. She was walking straight toward me. Sara and Bonnie from the Elite team were with her.

Suddenly my foot slipped. The book fell off my head. I wobbled. And then I fell right into the sandbox.

I can't believe this! I thought. *Lila Hanks is watching me do something totally embarrassing. Again.*

I picked my head up. There was sand in my hair. The little kids began to giggle.

Dana did, too.

"Are you okay?" Amanda called. But even she was smiling.

I was definitely not okay. I'd made a fool of myself in front of Lila Hanks twice in one day. And my friends thought it was funny! Everyone was laughing at me!

"No!" I said. "I'm *not* okay!" I tried to

climb out of the sandbox, and I banged my leg on the wooden corner.

"Katie — " Amanda began.

"Leave me alone!" I yelled. I burst into tears. "Both of you just leave me alone!"

I ran for my bike and pedaled away as fast as I could.

"Katie, wait!" Dana shouted.

"Come back!" Amanda called.

But I kept going. I didn't slow down till I got to the Good-bye Tree. Then I stopped. I could hear my friends riding behind me.

"You forgot your bag!" Amanda said breathlessly as she rode up. I took it from her.

"Are you okay?" Dana asked.

"No," I sobbed. "I don't want any more help."

Dana and Amanda glanced at each other nervously. "Are you mad at us?" Dana asked.

"No," I said. "But you aren't helping! I don't need to practice the backward moves I already know. And I don't need to work on my balance. I can't do the move because I'm *scared*. And you guys can't help me get un-scared. You have never been afraid of anything. You have no idea what it's like!"

My friends' faces looked blurry through my tears. I pulled my bag over my shoulder and rode away as fast as I could.

6
Positive Thinking

Thursday after school I went straight to the gym. I knew the only way to try the back walkover was to do it alone. If no one was watching me, I wouldn't be so nervous. I'd still be *scared*, but at least I wouldn't have to be embarrassed.

As I pedaled down the street, I repeated the same words over and over in my head: "I'll do a flip-flop on the beam today" and "I'll never be scared again."

Mom calls that "positive thinking." I know it *sounds* easy. But believe me, thinking positive thoughts is hard work. The bad ones keep butting in. Bad ones like "I'll never learn the move" and "Great gymnasts are *never* afraid."

When I got to the gym, I hurried to my locker.

I could hear voices coming from the little gym. I recognized one of them — Hannah Rose's. I groaned. Now I couldn't try the back walkover by myself. I peeked in to see who she was talking to. Lila Hanks!

Lila sat on the floor stretching her legs. Hannah Rose was telling her all about the Level 5 meet last month. She made it sound as if our team won because of *her*. Actually, it was mostly because of Dana and Amanda.

I sneaked back into the locker room. I didn't want Lila to see me. Not after yesterday. I changed quickly and quietly. Then I went into the big gym.

Coach Jody was busy on the mats with the Teeter Tots.

I turned to the balance beam. Dana

and Amanda were already there. They rushed right over to me.

This practice was definitely not going well — and it hadn't even started yet!

"Hi!" Amanda said.

"Hi!" Dana added.

"What are you guys doing here?" I asked.

"We've been thinking about what you said yesterday," Amanda told me.

"We decided you were right," Dana added. "We haven't been helping."

"But things are going to be different now," Amanda continued. "We understand your problem. And we really want to help."

"Thanks," I said. "But — "

"No buts," Dana broke in. She took hold of my arm and steered me toward the practice beam. But Emily and Liz were already working on it.

Why was *everyone* early to class the one time I needed to be alone?

"Rats!" I said. "I really wanted to practice before class."

"You still can," Amanda told me. "We'll use the high beam."

"But I haven't even done the move on the low one yet," I argued. "I don't want to start on the high beam!"

"Don't worry," Dana said. "We'll spot you."

"One on each side," Amanda agreed. "So you won't be scared."

My friends were really trying! Maybe they *could* help me after all.

"Well, okay," I said. "But you have to promise I won't fall."

"We promise!" they both answered together.

Before I could change my mind, Dana rushed to Coach Jody's place next to the high beam. Amanda went to the other side.

I told myself not to worry as I mounted the beam. Nothing could go wrong with both of my friends there. Right? I walked back and forth on the beam a few times to warm up.

"Okay," Dana said. "Go for it!"

"Don't rush her," Amanda said. "Take your time, Katie!"

I took a deep breath and wiped my sweaty hands on my leotard. "Okay," I told them. "I'm ready."

"Just lean over and do it!" Dana called.

I started leaning back.

"Wait!" Amanda cried.

I straightened up again. "What's the matter?"

"You forgot to point your toes," Amanda said.

"*A-man-da,*" Dana groaned. "That's not important."

"It is too!" Amanda said. "Katie should learn to do the move right!"

"How about just learning to *do* it first?" Dana argued.

"You guys!" I yelled.

"Sorry," Dana said.

"Sorry," Amanda agreed.

I took another deep breath. I pointed my right foot. Then I leaned back again. I saw the ceiling. Then I saw the wall. I still couldn't see the beam, so I leaned back even farther. And farther —

"More to the left!" Amanda told me.

"More to the right!" Dana called.

"Keep your back arched," Amanda said.

"Just grab the beam," Dana added.

I wobbled to the left and then the right. I arched my back. I tried to grab the beam . . . but I felt dizzy from being upside down for so long. I couldn't find the beam.

I was falling!

I hit the mat hard. I tried to breathe. But I couldn't. I put my head down between my knees. When I looked up again, Dana and Amanda were standing over me.

"Katie, are you all right?" Amanda asked.

Dana reached out a hand to pull me up. But I didn't take it. I stood up by myself. I was very mad at Dana and Amanda.

"You let me fall!" I cried.

Dana looked scared. "Katie — "

"Forget it!" I yelled. "You're just making everything worse!"

I turned and ran toward the door. I never wanted to see that dumb balance beam again!

"Katie!" Dana called after me. "Class is about to start."

"I don't care!" I yelled back. "I give up! I'm finished! I quit!"

7

A Secret

I was crying so hard I could barely see where I was going. I would never learn the back walkover on the beam. I would always be afraid of going backward. And if I couldn't stop being afraid, I would never be a great gymnast!

I dashed into the locker room. All I wanted was to be alone! But someone was sitting on the bench right by my locker. It was Lila Hanks.

Oh, no! I would be embarrassed in front of her again! I tried to sneak into the bathroom. But it was too late. Lila glanced up at me. Her blue eyes grew wide, and she jumped off the bench.

"Katie!" she cried. "What's wrong?"

I was so surprised I stopped crying. Lila Hanks knew my name?

"Katie?" she repeated.

"Um . . . it's nothing," I answered. "I was just upset."

"Come on, tell me," Lila prodded. "What's going on?"

Lila was being so nice that I started to cry again. I told her all about it. About being afraid. About how my friends kept trying to help me — and how they kept making things worse. About falling off the beam. I even told her how embarrassed I'd felt chickening out in front of her at the gym and then falling off the sandbox in the park.

"You sure are having a hard time," Lila said when I finished. "But you don't have to worry about *me*! I didn't even see you in the park. And I don't think you're a scaredy-cat."

"Even if I can't do a flip-flop on the beam?" I asked.

"Even then," Lila said. "But you *can* do it!" she added.

"I'm too afraid," I told her. "I should quit gymnastics. I'll never be any good."

Lila looked thoughtful. "I know just how you feel," she said. "You know, I almost quit once, too."

"You did?" I gasped.

Lila nodded. "Know why?"

I shook my head.

"Because I was afraid!" Lila said. "Of going backward!"

"No way!" I cried. "Really?"

"Really!" Lila said.

I tried to picture Lila Hanks being afraid. But I couldn't. "Do you still get scared?" I asked.

"Once in a while," she said. "But not much."

I sighed. "You're lucky."

"Luck has nothing to do with it," Lila said. "I know a secret."

"There's a secret?" I asked.

"Uh-huh. An older girl told it to me a long time ago," she said. "Suzanne Dillon."

I was so excited I jumped up off the bench. "Suzanne Dillon?"

Lila nodded.

Suzanne Dillon trained at Jody's Gym back before I even started gymnastics. Now she's at Jon Sokolov's gym in Texas. Everyone says she'll probably make the next Olympic team. She's my hero!

But I was confused. I sat back down next to Lila. "If Suzanne told *you*," I said, "that must mean . . ."

"Suzanne was scared to go backward," Lila finished for me.

Wow! I never would have believed it.

An Olympic hopeful — afraid to go backward.

"Can you keep a secret, Katie?" Lila asked me.

"Oh, yes!" I cried. Was she really going to tell me Suzanne's secret?

"Then come here," Lila said.

I moved closer to Lila. She leaned toward me. And then, just like that, she whispered Suzanne's secret in my ear.

My Buddy!

"Katie, you're late!" Coach Jody called.

"Sorry," I said as I ran into the gym.

I had been so busy talking to Lila that I missed the beginning of class. Warm-up was almost over.

Dana and Amanda were jogging around the gym side by side. I ran to catch up with them.

"We thought you weren't coming back," Dana told me.

"We were really worried," Amanda added. "And we're *really* sorry."

Dana nodded. "If we weren't fighting, you wouldn't have fallen."

"That's it for warm-up!" Coach Jody announced. "The Elite girls are here!"

Everybody turned toward the front of the gym, where the older girls were standing with Coach Jody.

I gasped. I'd been so worried about my back walkover, I'd completely forgotten that Tumbling Buddies was starting that day.

"Junior gymnasts, on the mats!" Coach Jody called out.

All the Level 5 girls plopped down on the floor. I squeezed in between Amanda and Dana.

Coach Jody glanced at a piece of paper she was holding. "Okay," she said. "Let's get started."

Amanda crossed her fingers and squeezed her eyes shut. I knew she was wishing for Lila Hanks as her buddy.

"Hannah Rose," Coach Jody began, "your Tumbling Buddy is Sara!"

Hannah Rose made a face.

To tell the truth, Sara didn't look too happy, either.

"Hannah Rose is so rude," Amanda whispered.

I nodded. But I noticed that Amanda had a little smile on her face. I knew she was glad Hannah Rose didn't get Lila.

"Amanda," Coach Jody went on, "your buddy is Leslie!"

Amanda stopped smiling. But she waved politely at Leslie.

"Sorry," Dana whispered to Amanda.

"Pay attention, Dana," Coach Jody said. "You're next!"

Dana bounced up and down on the mat. I could see her lips moving. "Lila, Lila, Lila," she was saying over and over again.

"Dana, your Tumbling Buddy is Bonnie," Coach Jody said.

Dana slumped down on the mat. I moved closer to her. "Bonnie's good, too," I whispered.

"Katie," Coach Jody went on, "your Tumbling Buddy is Lila!"

Dana turned to stare at me.

So did Amanda.

And so did Emily, Liz, and Hannah Rose.

I couldn't believe it! Lila Hanks was my Tumbling Buddy! Mine! It was too good to be true. But it *was* true.

Lila gave me a big grin and two thumbs up. I grinned back.

"You are *so* lucky," Amanda whispered.

"I know," I whispered back.

Dana nudged me. "Well, if I can't have Lila, I'm glad it was you," she said.

I hardly paid attention as Coach Jody matched up Emily and Liz. All I could think of was me and Lila Hanks working out together. Wow!

"Okay, team up with your Tumbling Buddies," Coach Jody called. "I want you to work on whatever the Level 5 girls need the most help with."

"Do you want to see my floor exercise?" I asked when Lila came over to me.

Lila laughed. "No way!" she said. "It's the balance beam for you."

I tried to relax as I climbed onto the practice beam. But as soon as I was up there, my heart began to pound. The rest of the girls were watching me. Dana and Amanda both looked worried.

But Lila smiled at me. "Just remember the secret," she said softly.

I nodded, feeling calmer already. *Suzanne Dillon used to be afraid of going backward, too,* I told myself. *Now she's practically in the Olympics.* I took a deep breath and thought about her secret. I leaned back.

This time I had no trouble seeing the beam behind me. I just reached back and grabbed it. Without stopping, I flipped my legs over my head. The next thing I knew, I was right side up! I couldn't believe it. Neither could anyone else!

Coach Jody clapped her hands.

Amanda and Dana cheered.

Even Hannah Rose smiled at me.

"Way to go, Tumbling Buddy!" Lila yelled.

I jumped off the beam, and my teammates crowded around me. But Lila interrupted.

"That was great," she said. "Now let's see it on the regular beam. Do you think you're ready?"

I nodded, and we moved toward the big beam. This time I didn't feel even a tiny bit scared! Now that I knew the secret, it was easy!

I mounted the beam. I didn't think about my balance. I didn't think about pointing my toes. I didn't think about *any-*

thing like that. Suzanne said the secret to a back walkover is not in your body. It's in your brain! The first step in doing the move is to imagine the *last* step — to imagine yourself *finishing* the walkover.

And that's exactly what I did! In my mind, I had just flipped over and I was standing tall, arms out, and smiling proudly. I kept imagining that as I did my flip-flop on the high balance beam. And then I wasn't imagining it anymore. I was doing it! I threw my arms out to the sides and smiled as I finished the move.

Everybody clapped again when I dismounted.

Amanda gave me a big hug. "Your toe point was perfect!" she said.

"So was your balance," Dana added. Then she gave *Amanda* a big hug. "I can't believe we did it!" she cried. "Amanda, we did it! We taught Katie the flip-flop!"

"You guys — " I started.

Dana held up a hand. "You don't have to thank us, Katie!" she said.

I turned to Amanda. "But — "

"It's okay," Amanda said. "That's what friends are for!"

She and Dana slapped high fives. I couldn't believe it! They thought their plans worked!

I wanted to thank Lila — her plan was really the one that worked! But before I could say anything, she put a finger to her lips and winked.

Maybe I should let Dana and Amanda think they really helped, I thought. Besides, I don't need to tell them about Lila's plan — *Suzanne's* plan.

That would be our secret. From one great gymnast to another . . . to another!

JUNIOR GYMNASTS

How important is winning?

Dana wants to win lots of ribbons at her first gymnastics meet. But when a new girl, Amanda, comes to Coach Jody's gym, Dana isn't the only star in the Junior Gymnasts class. Dana wants to beat Amanda more than anything. Is it OK to compete with a teammate?

Junior Gymnasts #1
Dana's Competition
by Teddy Slater

Handspringing in to a bookstore near you.

JRG1195

Be a Pony Pal!

Anna, Pam, and Lulu want you to join them
on adventures with their favorite ponies!

Order now and you get a free pony portrait bookmark and two
collecting cards in all the books—for you *and* your pony pal!

☐ BBC48583-0	#1 I Want a Pony	$2.99
☐ BBC48584-9	#2 A Pony for Keeps	$2.99
☐ BBC48585-7	#3 A Pony in Trouble	$2.99
☐ BBC48586-5	#4 Give Me Back My Pony	$2.99
☐ BBC25244-5	#5 Pony to the Rescue	$2.99
☐ BBC25245-3	#6 Too Many Ponies	$2.99
☐ BBC54338-5	#7 Runaway Pony	$2.99
☐ BBC54339-3	#8 Good-bye Pony	$2.99
☐ BBC62974-3	#9 The Wild Pony	$2.99
☐ BBC62975-1	#10 Don't Hurt My Pony	$2.99

Available wherever you buy books, or use this order form.

Send orders to Scholastic Inc., P.O. Box 7500, 2931 East McCarty Street,
Jefferson City, MO 65102

Please send me the books I have checked above. I am enclosing $_____ (please add
$2.00 to cover shipping and handling). Send check or money order — no cash or
C.O.D.s please.

Please allow four to six weeks for delivery. Offer good in the U.S.A. only. Sorry,
mail orders are not available to residents in Canada. Prices subject to change.

Name_____ Birthdate ___/___/___
     First   Last   M / D / Y

Address_____

City_____State_____Zip_____

Telephone (   ) _____ ☐ Boy   ☐ Girl

Where did you buy this book? ☐ Bookstore ☐ Book Fair ☐ Book Club ☐ Other

PP1295